THE CHOOSING

From The Memory Keepers

MARTA MORAN BISHOP

© 2011

ISBN: 978-1-939484-27-7

Crowe Press LLC

www.martamoranbishop.com

THE CHOOSING

MARTA MORAN BISHOP

This story is entirely fictional, any reference or similarity to any group or religion is only that the names that I used are real. However, this story is not based on any particular creed or religion but is a piece of my imagination. I took pieces of many different legends, religions, and beliefs and told a story entirely based upon a fictional tribe of people in a fictional world.

One

"Mondoani!"

"Yes, Old Mother."

"Your place is with me now. No longer will you sit with the young children or with the tribe – you are to be a memory keeper; the God's have chosen you.

Mondoani took a quick look at her friends at play before she solemnly followed Old Mother to the fire that separated them from the clan.

"You are not whom I would have chosen, Mondoani, for you are slight of body and frail in appearance. Perhaps, you will not be able to hold the spirits of the God's within you and survive the trance. However, they chose you, so I will teach you and we will hope you gain the physical and spiritual strength that is needed," the old mother said while gesturing for Mondoani to sit.

Mondoani said nothing; instead, she squared her small, thin shoulders and sat nearer to Old Mother's fire.

"Oh well, your body is not built for childbearing; maybe this is why they chose you. For the spirits of Sotunknang, the nephew of the great Creator; Takuskanskan, the God of change, themselves came down and picked you instead of the other young women. It was a remarkable and immense honor to be bestowed upon you.

From today forward, you will be called Young Mother as I was called in my youth and later, Mother. If you make it into old age as I have, your name, too, will be Old Mother."

"NO! Those were your names, but I will remain Mondoani. That is what the Thunder Boys yelled to me as they left the sacred place and even, Selu, the Goddess of the corn, named me Mondoani during the choosing. That is who I am and whom I will remain, Old Mother. I mean no disrespect, but I cannot bear your name."

The old woman sat speechless for a moment, taking in the words until acceptance filled her countenance.

"So be it!" she said. "Though it may be your downfall or your salvation, 'Mondoani' it is and 'Mondoani' it stays."

Outwardly, the young girl appeared calm but inwardly, she quaked and thought, *I had expected a bigger fight though I will not lose myself in the Old Mother. It would be the death of me, of that I am sure.*

With a last look of longing at her friends, she turned to the old woman. With great patience, Mondoani waited to take the next step forward into her new life. Her shoulder blades were thin, pronounced under a leather tunic, and large brown eyes filled her small face as she gazed at Old Mother. *This is the woman who will teach me, lead me, and be my world now,* Mondoani thought as she noticed for the first time the yellow of old age in the old woman's eyes. *Will there be time?*

"Mondoani, we have only a little time tonight for me to teach you about the power of the cacti, for tomorrow we will head out again into the dead lands. Nightfall must see us at the edge of the desert with the great cliffs in front of us."

Her quiet, ancient voice was nearly drowned out by the sound of the waterfall behind the camp. Yet, Old Mother's presence was still strongly felt by the tribe. Even the Chief, Concierce, glanced toward them at times. Everyone in the tribe looked to Old Mother for guidance and strength but did she have enough to make it through the next day?

"If Zoeantha had not fallen on the other side of the oasis, another choosing would not have been needed, but she did and here we are," continued Old Mother. "We must make the best of it. I hope you show as much promise as did Zoeantha, for she would have made an excellent memory keeper. Mondoani, age, has crept up on me; I fear my time is nearer than I wish it to be."

"Old Mother, please don't talk like that, it is surely too soon," Mondoani said to reassure.

"I sense that my passing time is near, Mondoani, and I have much to teach you before that time are upon us. Here, put some aloe on your face; it will help take the sun's heat from your skin." She said, handing the young girl a clay pot of clear salve.

"When you are finished, we will go and minister to those of the clan who suffer from the sun's burn."

After applying aloe to her own face, Mondoani placed the deer skin back atop the small clay pot and stood. She held the pot in her left hand; her right reached out to aid the Old Mother to her feet.

Taking Mondoani's hand, Old Mother rose and said, "When we have finished, you can bring me my supper for the ash cakes will be done and the women will have finished mashing the beans.

With luck, we will make it across the barren lands and to the cliffs tomorrow, but tonight we will sleep and gather strength for that journey."

"Old Mother, how long do you think it will be before the time of your passing draws near?"

"I believe we have a season or two, perhaps I will even make it through the time of the cooling before the snows come in. Mondoani, it is my last journey through the arid lands, of that I am sure."

"Will that be enough time, Old Mother? I fear that the knowledge you carry is too much to learn in so short a span.

"What I can teach you, I will, of that you can be sure. But one of the first things you will learn when we reach our home will be how to make the final transfer, should my time run out. I fear it will be a heavy burden for one so young." Even though the Gods always choose wisely. She said as they moved between the clan, each one receiving a measure of the precious aloe.

Two

The women of the tribe quietly handed out the remainder of last night's ash cakes and beans. In their eyes, Mondoani saw fear as they looked at the Old Mother. A few glanced at her in speculation though most avoided her eyes. *They are afraid I won't be able to take her place and they, too, see that age has crept up overnight on Old Mother,* she thought as she ate her cold breakfast between sips of water. Here, water was plentiful and all drank deeply before filling the skins with water. Each of them was aware that soon, the water would be rationed for there was only so much that could be carried; the dogs' loads must be light if they were to make it through the arid lands.

Father Sun had begun to peek over the horizon when the tribe set out. The most seasoned braves had already begun the trek. They would warn the clan if trouble developed, but few expected any this close to the warmer season.

Yet, the clan could afford no more losses. If the truth were to be told, the tribe could not afford the three they had lost on the other side of the oasis. One young woman close to birthing had died of fever and her baby with her; and, they had lost Zoeantha. The tribe was small and too few had joined it at the winter camp. Many of the other clans had also appeared to be diminished in strength from the year before.

Mondoani had heard much speculation about the plagues, poisoned water, and lack of rain during the past season. The old died and fewer were born to replace them. She, too, wondered why the Gods were angry with the clan and what could be done to appease them.

At the rear of the line, in front of the last of the braves, Mondoani walked with the Old Mother. Dawn had barely broken up from the horizon when the Old Mother faltered.

A hush fell as she put her shoulder under the old woman and helped her to her feet. If the Old Mother could not make it across the dead lands on her feet, Mondoani knew that the braves would carry her. Even should it mean the death of one of the braves, the Old Mother would be carried across the desert.

As the day wore on, however, the Old Mother grew in strength. She felt the spirits of the mountains and they filled her with their formidable power. The Old Mother's spirit guide was the element of Earth and her totem was the great black bear. Gone the weakness of her body, though it was still frail – the spirit of the bear sang through it now. She would live to reach their home. A quiet sigh filled the air around the clan as they moved through the desert, stopping only once to eat a small portion of left-over beans and take a tiny sip of water from the skins.

"Mondoani, come here," the old woman said as she walked over to one of the pale green cacti. "If you are out in the arid land and need water, you can find it here." Old Mother sank to her knees and raised her hands above her shoulders.

"Great Spirit of the Earth, I thank you for the bounty of this gift of water. I will take only what is needed and spare the cacti so it can continue to live," Old Mother intoned. "Watch Mondoani – your cut into the cacti must be slight and carefully done. You must not chop it or you will stunt the plant and maybe kill it."

"I see, Old Mother," Mondoani stated simply, her right hand underneath the old woman's hand. The stone blade sat heavily in her hand as the old woman guided her and together, they sliced into the cacti. A trickle of moisture ran down the prickly cactus and was caught in the clay pot the Old Mother held in her left hand.

Such had been the skill of the cut that, shortly, the cactus stopped bleeding its fluid.

"Thank you, Spirit of the Earth for this gift; we will use it wisely." The words of the Old Mother rang through Mondoani's soul. She felt both the bountiful gift of life flow through her and the departure of the spirit of the Earth, too.

Each of the tribe received a sip of the water from the cactus to aid them in the remainder of their journey. Their water skins had been growing empty so this bounty from the earth gave them sustenance where, otherwise, they might have needed to continue on thirsty. The oldest, the nursing mothers, and the smallest drank first and, finally, the remainder of the tribe. Mondoani was the last, licking the remaining moisture from the bottom of the dish.

All of the tribe knew Mondoani was the chosen one, but still the introduction ceremony had not been held. That would come after they settled into their home. Until then, she was neither of the tribe nor a memory keeper's apprentice.

In years past, the tribe only traveled away from their home once every few years to trade with the sea people or allow their braves to intermarry, thus rejuvenating both clans. However, because the lands around their home did not produce the food they once did it was necessary to winter elsewhere.

Mondoani knew that she leaving a part of whom she had been behind; who she would become was anyone's guess. *It feels as if I am separated from my childhood, my friends, and even myself in some kind of strange way,* she reflected as she moved up the path to the city.

Off in the distance, the tribe could see the faces of the cliffs hidden behind the murky haze of the desert sun. Yet, because they could see them at all meant they had moved past the halfway point in their day's journey.

A new eagerness filled the air as each of the clan recognized the truth and knew that their travels would soon be over. The power and majesty of the mountains was in front of them and, soon, they would go through the cliff passes to reach their cliffside dwellings. Strength and hope were renewed and reached deeply within to sustain the clan even though they still had many hours of travel in front of them. Still, they felt fortified with confidence.

The Old Mother's arm fell heavily upon Mondoani's shoulder as she leaned into it, her strength once again wavering. It had been a long day for the woman and even with the spirit of her totem bracing her, the old woman was spent.

It was good that the cliffs were close now, for if the braves needed to carry the old woman, none would die from exhaustion. It seemed all would survive now and make it home.

The blistering heat of the day would become icy cold as soon as the sun set, as is normal in the desert. The tribe must be in the shelter of the cliffs before nightfall as the change in temperature might be too much for the Old Mother. They could not afford to lose her, not yet, not now.

She must live to teach me and show me the way of the final transfer or the tribe will have no memory keeper, Mondoani thought fearfully. *I don't want to alert the braves to her condition if it is unnecessary. But, if I am too late we may lose her.* Mondoani thought, adjusting her shoulder, the weight of the Old Mother growing ever heavier. At least she was still able to pick up her own feet and put one in front of the other; they walked on.

The tribe struggled on through the heat of the afternoon without losing their resolved. The sight of the cliffs in front of them served only to fortify them.

Father Sun's glory lit up the sky just before it began to sink behind the mountains and then, the tribe entered the shadows of the cliffs.

The last of the braves ran forward, dancing and shouting as they stopped in front of the two women. With a bow to the Old Mother, the two strongest of the young men joined hands, making a chair to carry the old woman into the camp. She would enter the camp with ceremony for her life was precious to the tribe.

Even the dogs had managed to run the last few feet to the stream that ran beneath the cliff, the sleds still strapped to their backs. They were at the brook, lapping water thirstily. The young boys in the tribe were working to release the dogs before the leather straps became wet, impossible to untie.

Their young arms strained to keep both the sleds and the dogs out of the water.

Mondoani stumbled into camp at last. Nearly blind from exhaustion and thirst, she made her way to the edge of the stream then knelt down to drink and let the cool water run down her face and arms. Gathering a clay cup, she filled it with water to bring to the Old Mother.

I know I should have brought her the water first, but I don't know that I could have done so, she thought tiredly, making her way through the throngs of her people to the side of the old woman.

Three

"I am sorry I am late, Old Mother," said Mondoani, placing the cup into the old woman's hands.

"Not to worry my child; you half carried me at the end and for that I am grateful," Old Mother said as she touched Mondoani on the cheek, the first tenderness she had shown for her new apprentice. "Bring me my bedroll, please; I will nap a bit before we eat."

Mondoani rose and said, "Yes, ma'am. I will get it now. Would you like a bit of dried beef, too?"

"I am not hungry, only a little tired," said Old Mother. "Please hurry for I fear I will be caught napping, slumped here on the ground."

"I'll be right back," Mondoani said as she ran off to pull their packs from the sled and hurried back to take care of Old Mother.

As she rolled out the Old Mother's bedroll, helped her lie down upon it and covered her with a bearskin blanket, Mondoani sighed deeply and thought: *I am no longer a young girl; instead I am an apprentice though the ceremony has not yet taken place. My childhood is gone and the shroud of my new life is fully upon me now.* Mondoani's large brown eyes no longer searched for the friends of her youth. The mantel of loneliness was fully engulfing her.

Mondoani sat, though, smoothing the old woman's hair as she slept, keeping watch over Old Mother as she dozed. Her own arms ached and her belly rumbled with hunger. With patience, Mondoani relaxed and allowed the peace of the camp and the night air to fill her soul with its familiarity and beauty.

Almost of its own accord, her nose lifted and sniffed; the smells of the wood fire, the fried beans cooking, and the great birches high upon the hill filled her nostrils. The cold winds of the dead lands drifted through the camp, mingling with the scent of sweat, dogs, fresh water and food cooking. Mondoani's long black braids fell over her shoulders then as her head slumped and she, too, dozed. The Old Mother's thoughts swept into Mondoani's mind, mingling with her own and she began her second lesson. With a grunt and a shrug, the Old Mother woke; sleep left Mondoani at the first sound of the change in the old woman's breathing.

Life filled the air around them: the older children led the younger ones to the stream to wash. It was time to eat and then sleep for, tomorrow, the journey would begin and end again; both the homecoming ceremony and the ceremony to name her apprentice would take place at day's end.

It would be another long day, but a fulfilling one for the entire tribe. *At least the journey will soon be over,* Mondoani mused, *and our lives can begin again. I pray that this year the Thunder*

Gods and Thunder Boys bring rain. Perhaps, with the Old Mother's failing health, her power was also dwindling. If this is so, maybe she can pull from my essence and bring in the rain, teach me how to placate the spirits. We must have rain! She thought as she fell to sleep.

Dawn splashed across the sky; in the mountains, it came as quickly as did dusk. The dawn did not decline away as it did near the sea or in the prairies. Instead, in a matter of seconds, the sky changed from the blackness of the night to nearly full daylight.

Every member of the tribe was eager to reach their home so bedrolls were quickly rolled and, along with cooking utensils and pottery, were packed upon the sleds. The dogs, equally eager to reach home, stood basking in the daylight, panting and waiting for the young men to speak the words that meant for them to move.

The first of the braves left camp before daylight, moving up the slopes of the mountain side. The smell of bear hung in the air, though it was faint, the bear having passed further up days before. It, too, was moving to its summer home high up in the mountains. Still, a brave's eager eye and nose must keep watch for all manner of beasts that might still be on the prowl. Especially, if the winter had not been good to them and they were hungry.

Although tired, Mondoani had spent most of the night crafting a staff for the Old Mother. With her stone blade, rubbing stone, and a strong branch from a birch tree, she had made a handsome walking stick.

"Old Mother," she said quietly, shyly waiting for the old woman to look at her.

"Yes, Mondoani," said Old Mother.

"I have made you something," Mondoani said and she handed the staff to the old woman.

Running her hands along the staff, Old Mother said, "It is beautiful, Mondoani. When did you make it?"

"Last night, Old Mother."

"Did you sleep at all?"

"Just a little, but it was vital to me to finish making this for you. I hope you like it?" Mondoani asked, hesitantly.

Looking wonderingly at Mondoani, the Old Mother replied, "I promise you, I do; it means so very much to me that you spent your sleep time crafting this beautiful staff for me."

"I will sleep tonight then," Mondoani said, as a bright smile lit up her plain face.

Besides those large dark eyes, her smile is her best feature, the Old Mother thought warmly. *Perhaps, she will do better than I expected.*

"Let us move on then."

The white birch staff flickered brightly through the trees as the two women followed their clan up the mountain.

"Mondoani, this staff makes it much easier for me to walk. It is a brilliant and thoughtful gift.

Thank you," said the Old Mother, her stride steadier.

A blush swept slowly up the young girl's face and a hint of a smile lurked at the edge of her lips. It stayed there throughout the morning, growing brighter as the tribe drew closer to their home.

Overhead, an eagle circled and the tall spruce trees moved in a light breeze, a nice contrast against the bright blue spring sky. The worst of their travels behind them.

The cliffs could be difficult to climb, but their feet felt light, so close to the end of their travels. Before them stood the cliffs, sandstone dwellings built into the caves. The white of sandstone and the red of the adobe adorned the buildings and made them glitter in the sunlight.

"Home at last!" said the Old Mother with a sigh of relief.

"Yes!" Mondoani breathed in a breath of fresh air and let out a sigh of relief. Though, all of a sudden, she was unsure where she lived in this city.

"Old Mother?" she asked.

"Yes, Mondoani."

"Where is my home now?"

"Oh dear girl, you have a room in my house, over there near the main Kiva," Old Mother said, pointing up to the right of the gleaming city. "That will be our home and one day, your home. It is quite large with storage in the higher levels and a courtyard of its own for cooking, making pottery, doing lessons; our own kiva where we practice our trade. Lucky for me in my old age, the ladders and paths to our home are short and not as steep as some of the others."

"It is quite a distance from the main part of the city isn't it?" asked Mondoani, staring up in the direction the Old Mother pointed.

"Yes, Mondoani; sometimes it gets lonely but one tunes into the sounds of life, silence from the tribe, and the beauty that comes from being closer to the spirit world. It can be a full life if you let it," spoke Old Mother.

"I suppose so, Old Mother," she said sadly.

"You will see, dear," continued Old Mother."You will learn to open yourself to much more than the noise of the tribe. Give my way of life a chance; it is glorious in its own kind of beauty."

From their trek through the arid lands, across the Great Plains, and through the forest lands, both Old Mother and Mondoani had suffered many blisters. Their woven shoes made from the yucca plant, although sturdier than most things, had seen better days. The soles were paper thin in places and, here and there, a small hole appeared. Mondoani knew that one of her roles as an apprentice would be to make them both new shoes; this would be done while the Old Mother taught her other things, such as, the names of plants: those that healed insect bites, ones that helped babies who were teething, and those that kept infections out of the wounds that braves suffered when they went to hunt.

But tonight, after the sun sank and the stars lit up the sky, the ceremonies would take place.

The torches would be lit and the spits filled with cooking meat, its fat dripping into the fire; and the scent of the spruce trees would fill the air.

Mondoani knew the women would be cooking in the main courtyard. The braves would be out hunting and the older children both sweeping out the rooms and running errands. In the past, she had a part in all of these preparations, but now she felt at loose ends. The Old Mother had gone to nap and after that, she would make ready for the ceremony. *What is my place in this now?* She thought, feeling somewhat despondent.

Four

After the Old Mother awoke, she and
Mondoani made their way down to the stream.
They bathed in the herbal waters, rubbed oil of
lavender and sage into their skin until they both
glowed and then both women sat upon stone stools
and brushed their hair. Mondoani helped the Old
Mother braid her gray streaked hair with bits of
turquoise and lava, the teeth of the wild boar, and
bits of crystal beads.

Mondoani had few ornaments to braid into her
hair, but its dark lush color had its own beauty.
The time would come when she, too, would braid
her hair with bits of stones, adorning it in the
fashion of the Old Mother's; but tonight was only
the beginning of her new life.

When both women had finished and Mondoani
had helped the Old Mother dress in her finest

tunic, she was given a new leather tunic by the Old Mother.

It was the finest dress she had ever owned and would serve her well. Its front was covered in beading, with pieces of black lava and light and dark turquoise; it fell past her knees, nearly hitting the floor of the main room.

Their feet now adorned with shoes made of the yucca plant, woven into sandals and decorated with bright colored stones and beading, Mondoani thought the time had come. Instead, the Old Mother handed her a cup of amber liquid. The heady smell of the honeyed corn liquor filled the air of the room.

The Old Mother spoke, "Tonight you become, in the eyes of the tribe, my apprentice and, soon, the second memory keeper. The tribe has only known me for I have lived long and through many generations of chiefs.

But, in reality, you have been my apprentice since the moment that the Gods chose you, Mondoani. I drink to you, your future, and to us."

The old woman raised up her cup, tapped the side of Mondoani's and then, both women drank deeply. The sound of drums rang through the air, calling them to the courtyard.

"It is time!" The old woman said, picking up her birch staff and walking out into the darkness of the night.

Lit only by the torches held by the children and the braves standing along the path, lighting the way for the two women, Old Mother and Mondoani followed the path to the courtyard.

In the courtyard, Chief Concierce stood with his wife, Naomi, at his side; the Chief was dressed in his finest leather tunic and fringed pants.

A tall feathered crown lay upon his head, his black hair loosely held in place by bits of gems and herbs tied into it here and there.

The drums beat louder and incense filled the air, mixing and melding with the smells of the feast that was still cooking.

The courtyard filled with each man, woman, and child – young and old alike. All were dressed in their best, with hair brushed, braided, and adorned, but none so richly done as Concierce, Old Mother, and Mondoani.

As the two women reached the center of the circle, Naomi left her husband's side and moved to the outside of the circle. Old Mother took her place beside Chief Concierce and they stood side by side, with Mondoani in front of them.

Old Mother and Concierce began the chant:

"To the guardians of old, we thank you for blessing us with a safe trip back to our home."

"The guardians of the spirits of Earth, Air, Fire, and Water, although we lost some on our trip, we also gained; they will not be forgotten. Thank you for giving unto us one who will one day be our memory keeper and keep our feet in the light."

The chant grew bolder and louder, the drums beat stronger and heavier. At the crescendo, the sound of a single flute filled the air, lifting each soul higher and into a richer, closer plane.

"I give you Mondoani, as the chosen of the Gods to be both apprentice to Old Mother and one day, our memory keeper," said Concierce.

A murmur moved through the crowd, each person wishing to gossip with their friends and family.

Of course, they all were at the choosing, yet none had been able to spare neither the time nor energy during their journey to gather and thoroughly speculate about Mondoani.

Five

Spring became summer and still the Thunder Boys and Thunder Gods had not come, nor did they bring rain. The Old Mother taught Mondoani how to cast a circle properly and call the Gods.

She learned how to smell the air for any hint of rain, snow, and sand; and how to identify the smell when beasts drew close enough for the braves to hunt.

Mondoani was taught how to tease the corn so that it would grow in spite of the lack of water.

With deep sadness and fear she watched the Old Mother began to lose her ability to go into the trance.

More often than not, the Old Mother watched over Mondoani when she entered the trance.

It became obvious that the Old Mother's blood grew thinner. It could be seen in the amount of gray streaked hair that she lost each day and how heavily she leaned on her white birch staff.

The same staff that Mondoani had carved for her so many moons ago. With the passage of time Mondoani watched the Old Mother's hands shake and her step become less steady.

Still, the Old Mother taught Mondoani even as the heat of summer turned into fall. Both were aware that their time together was growing short; the Old Mother was failing rapidly now.

"Mondoani, I fear soon it will be my time to go into the final trance," said the Old Mother one morning.

"Please, don't say that Old Mother for I am not ready," Mondoani stated, visibly shaken.

"It is the way of things, my daughter," Old Mother said, tucking a stray piece of Mondoani's hair back into her braids. "I didn't expect you to be the one chosen nor did I anticipate that I would learn to care for you so deeply.

You have done well, Mondoani, yet I know there is so much I will not have time to teach you before my time will end."

"NO! Old Mother, please don't say that," said Mondoani, grasping the Old Mother's hands.

"Don't cry dear," responded the Old Mother, hugging Mondoani, "for it is the truth and, before another day has drawn to an end, I must teach you the ceremonial tasks for the final transfer. Allow peace to enter your spirit, my daughter, and smell the spruce trees. They are different today."

"Why do they smell different Old Mother?" Mondoani asked, quizzically, her attention turned.

"The spruce trees are beginning the process of going to sleep for the winter. Their sap is growing thicker and it is moving more slowly in their limbs," responded the Old Mother.

"Yes, I can smell it," said Mondoani, her head raised, sniffing the air.

"I understand now, but why is this relevant to the last transfer, Old Mother?"

"I will explain momentarily," replied the Old Mother.

Satisfied for the moment, Mondoani stated, "Old Mother, I fear we will have to make the trek through the arid lands once more; again, we have not been able to grow enough food for the tribe to put away any winter stores."

"I believe you are correct in this, Mondoani," Old Mother said, nodding her head. "There may come a time when the tribe must move to the plains and find a new path, one where we never need return again to this city in the caves. For without rain, the tribe cannot continue to survive here. It will be your task to help them build a new life elsewhere."

"Old Mother, do you think the tribe will follow me? I am so young and untested," said Mondoani, hesitant and unsure.

"Daughter of my heart, I believe you will prove you are more than worth their trust. Perhaps, it is because my end time is near and I can no longer call the rain," revealed the Old Mother. "If that is so, it is possible that, when you are the memory keeper, the Thunder Gods will come again."

"Do you believe that one loses their ability to call upon the Gods when one is at the end of their days, Old Mother?" asked Mondoani.

"I do not know, Mondoani. It is possible but come, I must teach you how to reach through my last trance and find my memories and the memories of all the memory keepers from the dawn of time. This teaching must not wait," spoke the Old Mother. "It must be now for night is coming quickly and my strength is waning."

During the coming weeks the Old Mother slept more often and in her waking hours she only taught Mondoani what was absolutely necessary.

She taught those things that would help the young woman sort through the eons of memories that would come to her during the final transfer.

Six

Mondoani wiped the Old Mother's brow and brushed her thin, gray streaked hair, thinking about her future. *It is near her time. She has laid in this trance for three days and four nights now. Soon, I will be the new memory keeper and it is a fearful thing. There is still too much to learn. Is it possible for me to reach her in the trance? If I can't, is it still possible for the final transference of power and knowledge to come to me before she passes into the next world?*

Mondoani's body was stiff from sitting so long in the same position, tending the Old Mother without food and only a bit of stale water to carry her through. *I know that no one can enter the kiva until I call them when the Old Mother's body has died, but how long can I go on without food and sleep?* She wondered, struggling to find some ease.

A small sigh escaped the Old Mother's lips – it *is time*, Mondoani sighed, placed her temple to the Old Mother's forehead and went into the trance. All the old woman's memories and stories, the rituals and histories that she had not yet taught Mondoani came flooding into her, along with the regrets, hopes, and fears that were the Old Mother's. Mondoani tensed as she felt the Old Mother's sadness about the children she had never born, for the years of loneliness she had as she watched one tribe member after another pass into the Summerland before her. All these feelings flooded into Mondoani and she sagged with the weight of them.

She walked beside the Old Mother when she had led the tribe through the darkness of the forests and watched as massive black bears tried to steal food from the tribe and when wolves howled at the edge of the campfires.

Mondoani's body began sweating with the heat that beat down on her as she walked along trails through arid lands and, as she moved through the thoughts of the Old Mother's. Mondoani's own heart broke a little with each loss that the Old Mother had suffered.

At the final beat of the Old Mother's heart, the last of the rituals and histories poured into Mondoani – so many that her mind could not sort them out at this time; *maybe I will never be able to*. Mondoani thought and for the last time, she smoothed the old woman's hair. Stumbling to her feet, weak with fasting, Mondoani made it to the flap that served as a door and opened it, startled by a figure that stood at the door.

"How long have you waited Naomi?" she whispered, spent.

"Two days and three nights, Mondoani," said Naomi, holding out a bowl towards Mondoani. "I have a bit of tortilla to break your fast and some fresh water. You must be terribly hungry."

Grasping the bowl, Mondoani gestured with her head and said, "That I am. Come in. It is time to ready the Old Mother so she may enter the Summerland."

Naomi stood at the entrance, fearful to move further into the room, so in awe had she been of the Old Mother. Even though she had known her since birth and the Old Mother had helped her with the birth of her daughter, Ashtra, Naomi stood in a near trancelike state, afraid to enter the holy sanctuary of the Old Mother.

Mondoani finished the tortilla, washed it down with the fresh water, and freshened up her hands and face before turning back to Naomi.

"We have much to do to prepare the Old Mother and little time, Naomi," she said, taking out the herbs that would be used to bathe the Old Mother and the oils that they would massage into her skin.

"I'll go and get the water. It won't take me long," Naomi said, disappearing out of the room.

"Old Mother, the tribe is not ready to lose you. I don't know if they will accept me, as young and untried as I am," Mondoani spoke timidly as she smoothed a bit of her own black hair back into its braid. Her statement was met with emptiness and a shudder of terror swept over her.

Concierce, the chief and shaman of the tribe, could be counted on for wise counsel. Still Mondoani knew there would be much for her to prove, and that her questions must not be seen as immature or reckless.

The customs of the tribe did not allow for her to make any decisions until the Old Mother had fully passed into the next world. The tribe was at a standstill and winter was rapidly approaching.

Neither in the memories of the Old Mother or in her own memory could she think of a time when the tribe had not already started their journey to the south. She feared; yet as the death of the Old Mother drew near, they could only wait out this time of insecurity. Without a memory keeper, the tribe could not move forward, and she could not take her place until the Old Mother had gone through that final door. That was the way of things, and now she stood and pulled all those things that had been learned out of her mind.

When the time came she must check for all of the signs that had been taught her. She must be sure or the tribe would not accept her in the future and they would all be doomed.

Naomi reentered the room carrying a large clay pot of water. Together, they washed the old woman's body in herbal water, massaged sage and lavender oils into her skin, and dressed the Old Mother in her best ceremonial garments. They braided her thin gray streaked hair with feathers, the rarest of herbs and dried flowers, and clasped a necklace of crystals, turquoise, and hardened lava around her neck. When they were finished, Naomi, wife of Concierce, bowed her head low and silently left to notify the rest of the tribe to begin the funeral preparations.

Mondoani washed herself, dressed in her best clothing, and re-braided her hair with turquoise, feathers, and lavender before she knelt and prayed to the gods for guidance. During her prayers, she swayed with exhaustion.

The braves finally arrived to carry the Old Mother's body to the funeral pyre, where they placed her with care upon the platform woven from hemp. Her personal belongings were placed around her so everyone in the Summerland would know her worth.

Every member of the tribe stood had gathered. Even the babies in their cradleboards on the backs of their mothers were in the circle around the altar, waiting for the chief to put a flame to the platform, and for the chanting to begin.

The time of Old Mother's final passing was at hand, though none of them remembered the last time; none present had been born when the last memory keeper had been ushered through the final door. Mondoani stood near Concierce as he lighted the funeral pyre.

The smells of burning hemp, wood, incense, and cloth filled the air, mingling with the sweet odor of the oils and herbs that saturated the skin of the Old Mother; these would mask the smell of her burning flesh.

One by one, each clan member moved forward and told a story from their own memory of a time they had with the Old Mother. All of the clan's recollections would honor the Old Mother and help her to bridge the gap from this world into the Summerland.

Chief Concierce and Mondoani led the song. The sound of the clan's voices moved up and down in waves, and was held together with the beats from many tom-toms. Toward nightfall, the chanting reached new heights and rang out through the night air, over the cliffs, and up to the stars themselves.

No one moved; they all stood until the last of the flames died and the Old Mother's body had become dust. When the spirit of the Old Mother had gone through that final door, the exhausted tribe sat together under the stars. They chewed on a bit of dried corn tortillas, dried beef, cold beans, and fed their babies before they sought their sleeping places.

Seven

Before she had reached puberty, the Old
Mother had picked Mondoani to study the history
of all the generations before. She had learned how
to read the signs of the weather, the spirits, and the
precise time to act for the good of the tribe.
Mondoani could understand the specific moment
when her people should pack up and move to
warmer land. If one were trained, the time to move
could be smelled in the air and seen in the fast
movements of birds as they flew south. If the signs
were read wrong, then the entire tribe would suffer
from what could be a disastrous early or late move.

Her black hair flowing down her back,
Mondoani stood watching the faint light come up
over the horizon of the desert beyond the cliffs.

With a black shawl pulled tight around her shoulders, Mondoani watched her breath in the early morning haze.

The cold was coming. It could be smelled in the nearness of the beasts of the north, and the wind held the scent of wild storms from the arid land and the prairie beyond. *We have been here too long,* she thought. *Yet it had been crucial to complete the week-long mourning ceremonies for the old woman. To dishonor her memory and life would have led to further disaster. The universe protects those who had lived as one with it and who honored all. The Old Mother had lived longer than anyone else in the tribe and had spent her life in service of the Gods, the land, the animals, and the tribe.*

Now the burden of the tribe's future was Mondoani's responsibility as the new memory keeper.

It was her job to help Concierce lead the tribe and read the signs. If she chose wrongly, then they could run into severe snow storms or the beasts of the night that prowled on the edges of the barren winter land.

If the worst happened, the tribe would lose the young and the old in the process. If they moved on too early, they might fail and not add to their stores; one more hunt could make their survival on the trip easier and might mean life and death to some.

Mondoani remembered the Old Mother's warnings about the beasts that prowled the forests and prairies, about the snakes and scorpions that filled the desert. She did not know if any of the worst beasts still lived, for they had not been seen in many years; yet to discount their existence could be death to all of them.

The tribe was not large enough to survive the loss of anyone. They could not afford to lose even one of the women heavy with babies or the young who would learn to fight, to hunt, and ultimately, to grow the tribe.

Each life was dear to the tribe and it was now her duty to keep them safe.

Mondoani found happiness in her ability to teach the next generation and to tell the stories of their past at the celebrations. At times, this was a heavy burden, yet she had been trained well by the Old Mother even though their time together had been short. The Old Mother had many other apprentices before Mondoani had been picked. All of them had passed on before the Old Mother and thus, had never become memory keepers. Because of this, Mondoani was the last apprentice chosen.

She had been picked when younger than most and thus, had fewer years to learn her craft before the passing of the Old Mother. *I am afraid*, Mondoani thought; *am I ready?*

She stood quietly, smelling the air and watching the first light break over the horizon.

With care, she watched for any traces that would give her the signs she had been taught would help her to make the right decision for the tribe. When she caught sight of early morning geese taking off in a fast flight south, Mondoani knew she was right: The tribe should have started their journey a week ago. They must act quickly and be on the trail today, the earlier the better. Each hour might be the difference between survival and death.

Taking a deep breath, Mondoani pounded the small drum to rouse the tribe from slumber. They had little time and must hurry now.

Eight

Setting her shawl more firmly around her shoulders, she set to work packing up those tools that she had used to help her invoke the proper Gods and open her mind to see all the correct signs. With care, she rolled up the rosemary, lavender, lilac, sage, and bat wings and placed the packet into her pouch. Leaving the center of her circle, she walked to the north corner and picked up the piece of black lava and the woven shield that signified the element of earth. "To the Element of Earth, I release you and ask you to protect our people in our quest for a new land."

Even though deep in the trance, she walked to the east. *It all must be done correctly to ensure the safety of our journey*, she thought and picked up the piece of yellow quartz and the stone knife. "To the Element of Air, I release you and ask you to hold off the winter winds as we journey to the south."

Mondoani continued on to the southern corner and picked up the piece of red coral and the wooden staff lying on the bare brown earth. "To the Element of Fire, I release you and ask you to protect us with health and cooler sunlight on our travels."

Finally, she reached the western corner and stooped down. Carefully, she picked up the piece of turquoise and the wooden cup that were there. "To the Element of Water, I release you and ask you to help us reach the shores of the great sea and aid us in finding water when we need it."

Each stone was placed in a cloth pouch. The knife, staff, cup, and woven shield were wrapped and replaced in their proper pouches. The whole was then rolled up and carried into her small curtained place inside the cave. There, she quickly packed the rest of the precious tools of her trade and the herbs that would heal the rot from the cold or the wounds of battle. Even the little things that would provide comfort to a new baby getting its first tooth were packed along with the few personal items she had; most of the things that the Old Mother used in the past had been added to the funeral pyre. *I will have to make do until I can gather my own tools,* she thought.

With the heavy bundle on her shoulders, Mondoani joined the tribe as it began its journey to the south. The women carried their babies in cradleboards on their backs. Older children walked alongside the dogs as they pulled the sleds loaded with the tribe's belongings, food, and water. The men carried their weapons at ready.

Scouts had been sent out a few hours before the tribe began their expedition. These men were the fastest and the bravest of them all, for if there were trouble they would need to warn the clan. Each of them had been equipped with a small drum, a flute, a spear, knife, and a club. The drum and the flute were to alert the tribe before one of them could reach it. The spears, knives, and clubs might protect them should they run into something dangerous. Perhaps they would need to defend themselves or the braves might find a bit of fresh meat to supplement the tribe.

Chief Concierce led them and he was followed by his sons and then the women and children. *My job is to watch and make sure none fall or become ill. I must watch the signs and make sure the tribe takes the correct path to get to our winter home and set the proper protections around them as we journey. It is for this reason I am toward the rear of our group, s*he thought settling her thoughts in order.

Behind Mondoani were the last of the braves. It was their job to protect those who were just past puberty, untried in the real arts of survival but now considered as men of the tribe. These young braves were the smartest and most skilled of their generation and they must live to carry on as their

fathers and uncles became too old to hunt and
fight.

As the tribe walked, Mondoani thought about
all of the knowledge that she had received at the
final transfer of power from the Old Mother. She
was surprised to learn that there were things the
Old Mother had not known and this frightened her.
So many of the memories that now filled her mind
spanned eons of time and each memory must be
available for her to call upon if needed. So much
had changed for the tribe in these last few months,
due to the Thunder Gods not bringing rain. *I must
be ready for things that have not been needed in
generations but will become necessary for me to
know,* she thought, determined to be ready for
anything.

Mondoani realized now just how many things
filled her brain; many had not been used or called
upon by the Old Mother in her time as memory
keeper. The knowledge spanned so many
generations that even the Old Mother did not know

how ancient the memories were or when they began.

I prefer to think about the joyful stories and the lessons that I will teach the children, Mondoani thought, and her face showing a hint of a smile. She loved the children and loved to watch them at play. Memories of her own childhood play swept over her then as she watched the little ones in the arms of their mothers or as they followed the tribe holding each other's hands.

Although her own childhood had been cut short when the Old Mother had picked her, Mondoani's regrets were few. She was chosen by the Gods and the Old Mother had been only a conduit. The tribe could not survive without a memory keeper. Soon, she would have to choose an apprentice from among the little ones and, for a moment, wished that memory keepers were allowed to have children. This same regret she knew was one the Old Mother had lived with.

All at once, Mondoani stopped in her tracks. *All the children of the tribe are mine*, she thought, now smiling widely. *I wonder if the Old Mother also understood this.* Mondoani walked on and pondered these revelations. Soon, she began to wonder: who would remember the children's stories? Who would remember their play in the future? Maybe she should add the children's stories to the histories that would be passed down to the next memory keeper. For without memories of play, life could be too heavy a burden in their harsh world.

Toward dusk, the tribe stopped; by then, everyone was hungry for breakfast had been only a cup of water and a piece of dried buffalo – they had eaten as they walked. They built their camp along the back edge of a cliff. Tomorrow the tribe would have to head out into the open land without the protection of the cliffs but, tonight, they could sleep easily; guards would be placed to watch for predators. They would be rotated to give each a portion of sleep for tomorrow's journey would be long. They must make it through the arid land. Mondoani's fear rose; it was time for her to go cast the Circle of Fortification around the tribe and call the spirits to guide and protect them through the dead lands that lay before them.

While the women cooked, they kept the little ones near them; no one spoke, for all felt the ingathering of power and feared the next day's journey. Each knew that a year without rain would have made the arid lands worse. Many cacti would have perished for even they needed some water, but the underground rivers were drier this year.

As the older children tended the fires, unpacked from the sleds what would be needed that night, and fed the dogs, the men hunted for what game could be found this close to the desert. If they were lucky, they would come back with a few prairie dogs or a rattlesnake. It was not much for the entire tribe, but combined with the dried corn and herbs, that would cook up nicely. Best of all, the tribe could save their stores for another day.

It is my job to call upon the Gods so that they may aid the tribe on the next part of our journey, Mondoani thought as she walked away from her people to seek a secluded place to cast her circle. Prior to her meditation, she called on the Four Quarters. Her trance must be deep and yet, she must remain protected.

"In the past, it was my job to watch over the Old Mother when she was in the trance. But, since I have no assistant, I must make my own protection and it must be strong enough to protect me while in my trance, as well as protect the tribe. I can do this," Mondoani whispered. *I am prepared,* she thought and, though frightened, finished lighting the fire and casting her circle before she sank to the ground. *I am ready* was the last thought before she sunk into her trance and joined the spirits of the universe in order to lay the protective spell around her people.

The stars had lit up the sky by the time that the trance lifted; a chill swept through Mondoani as she reentered the world. The Circle of Protection had been cast. As Mondoani stood, her legs trembled and she thought, *I must eat, and soon. Before this trip is over I'll need to pick an apprentice. It took too much of my energy to hold the protection around myself while in the trance. I need someone who can protect me while in the trance; if should something happen to me, my people would not be defenseless.*

Mondoani repeated her ritual backwards, opened the circle and released the Quarters before packing up her tools and returning to the camp.

Nine

Though she stumbled a little, with the aid of her staff Mondoani managed to make it into camp – to the fire. Her stomach grumbled at the smell of food and she thought, *I will wait to put away my tools until after I eat.*

"Mondoani," Naomi said, waiting by the fire.

"It is done, Naomi. We are protected this night," said Mondoani, swaying before the fire.

"You are too tired for one so young," said Naomi, concern on her face. "Is it because you do not have an apprentice? You must pick one of the girls and soon. What would happen to us if we had no memory keeper, no one to speak to the Gods for us and no one who remembers the traditions of our people?"

"You are right, Naomi," responded Mondoani. "I will begin watching the girls. I don't wish to select one as young as I was when I began training, for it's a hard life and it is made harder by no childhood. Yet, the girl that is picked must be young enough to learn quickly. I'm not nearing the end of my life as the Old Mother was when she picked me so, perhaps, a young woman can be found who will suit us all."

"Please don't take my Ashtra. I fear she would not suit you, nor can I bear losing her." Naomi said wringing her hands.

"I cannot make you any promises for the Gods will tell me who is to become my apprentice, Naomi," said Mondoani, placing a hand on Naomi's shoulder. "For all it is worth, I don't believe Ashtra is suited either. Being an apprentice is a lonely life for a young girl and Ashtra is remarkably social. As is the custom, the choosing will take place in the holy place at the oasis."

Naomi nodded her understanding and, after helping Mondoani to sit beside the fire, she gave her a bowl of food.

Ten

Mondoani ate and watched the children at play. Most of them should have been asleep by now, but their mothers were busier than normal tonight.

Tired yet somewhat restored by the food, she mused about a way to calm the children for sleep. *Perhaps I could tell them a story? It would serve multiple purposes to do so. For one thing, it would settle them down, and for another, it would help me to see which of the girls might be candidates for the choosing. I believe I will recognize the one who is to be my apprentice, by the way she listens and what her eyes tell me as the words of the story spin through her.*

Whoever is to be the apprentice will show certain signs that only Mondoani could notice, signs that they are becoming one with the story.

It would not be the same for the others watching; they would see all the children as if watching them at play. For, although most people show signs of emotion when hearing stories, the girl to be chosen would become a part of the story. *All these things might help me pick who would stand at the choosing,* Mondoani thought. *I will need many candidates for the Gods to select from.*

As she stood and brushed the crumbs from her leather dress, Mondoani again looked at the children. *How could I pick one, rip a young girl from her mother and bring her into such responsibility? The girl I pick will lose her childhood,* Mondoani thought sadly as she bent over, picked up her pouch, and walked over to her bedroll. Someone had laid it out neatly for her and placed her belongings carefully to the side, a bowl of water nearby to wash herself.

With a small smile, Mondoani rinsed the dust of the trail from her hands and face, and turned once again towards the children. With care, she pulled her stones from the pouch in her pocket and fingered them while her brain pondered. *Which story should I tell? How I dread this burden, though it must be faced. What will happen if none of the girls is the right one?* Shaking free of her thoughts, she walked over to the fire and spoke.

"Children, why don't you gather round and I will tell you a story before you sleep." Excitement lit their young faces as the children quickly moved toward her, asking questions as children do.

"Mondoani, would you tell us about the eagle tonight?"

"What's your name, young man?"

"Saret," he said simply.

"Well, Saret," Mondoani said with a smile, "Tonight will be different for the Gods have chosen the story," she said with surprise and thought: *That is not what I was going to say.*

A look of disbelief crossed their faces, for it was the custom for children to pick their own bedtime stories.

"Let us start a new tradition tonight. I think you will like it because you will learn so much more than before. Life can be full of wonder and mystery, but if we only hear the same stories and no new ones, we lose so much of that mystery." *Where are these words coming from?* Mondoani thought, her eyes widening in surprise. *Not one of the words I am speaking is what I meant to say.*

"Which story will you tell, Mondoani?" the children cried in unison, eyes wide with amazement.

"I'm going to tell you about Sky Spirit, the God who came down and entered the Sipapu. It is there that our people entered this world and became who we are today," she replied, gazing around at each child.

A hush fell over the children. The women stopped what they were doing, and even the men guarding the camp and those resting from their labors began to pay attention. The night air seemed to gather strength and became filled with the spirits of the Gods and of the tribe's ancestors. It was unusual for children to be told about the Sipapu though most knew the story about the Kiva. Even the older members of the tribe had never seen the true Kiva, only the replicas that men had made.

Legends said the one true Kiva was far out in the dead lands, buried these many generations.

Eleven

With her first words, the flame from the fire grew larger; the fingers of flame reached for the sky and the very air became thick with haze. The darkness of the night became heavy with the ingathering of spirits and then, the cliffs behind the camp disappeared. The very stars vanished behind the gathering mist. Softly the wind wailed and an eagle screeched as Mondoani began.

"A beautiful shining creature named Sky Spirit flew down into the Sipapu and entered the third world. There, he took a woman from that world as his wife. Her hair was long and black as night and her eyes were the color of new grass; they twinkled with the light of the stars. Her name was Spider Woman."

All eyes were upon her now, for none had heard this story before. She had only learned of it with the final transfer of power at the passing of the Old Mother. So buried in the eons of memories that now lay in her mind, Mondoani had not been aware that this story was known to her.

She continued: "The third world was filled with much wickedness. Men and women were not living in true harmony with the Gods. They did not honor the earth or the animals. Few respected one another. Sky Spirit could not live in a world so destroyed by man, so wrought with pestilence, famine, disgrace, and dishonor; so he said to his bride, 'We must fly from here to the fourth world and build a new one.'

'Husband," said Spider Woman, 'where is the fourth world, and how do we get to it?

My heart is yours, and my belly will soon be swollen with child. I don't wish the child to be born without you.'

'I have a gift for you my beloved,' Sky Spirit said as he handed her a long reed.

'Husband, what can I do with this?'

'You must enter it and I will carry you through the third world and into the fourth. All those whose hearts are filled with the love of all that is may come with us and begin a new life.'

"Spider Woman gathered all those of the clan together. Only those that were strong of faith and fierce in their love of what was good, natural, and at one with the Gods would be chosen. Sky Spirit was adamant that none whose hearts held wickedness and hatred would be chosen. So it was that, with extraordinary care, Spider Woman spoke only to those of her people that she knew to be of like mind and heart.

To these she offered the chance to make the trip into the fourth world.

"These people were all fearful for trust had long been difficult in their land—a land whose air held poisons, its waters full of the dead and dying, and its ground arid, no longer able to produce enough food for everyone. Father Sun had been harsh in the third world for many years and Mother Rain did not come; nor did the Thunder Gods or the Thunder Boys. Sky Spirit was more of a stranger to the people, though he was beautiful to look upon—so beautiful that his presence lifted their spirits. And so it was that they agreed to follow Spider Woman and Sky Spirit to the fourth world.

"The first to enter the reed was Spider Woman, for Sky Spirit believed she must enter the new world first or disaster could strike.

It would take a woman with the essence of life to exist in the arid land and one whose very breath could blow fresh air into the new world. She would be the one who could negotiate with the beasts of the fourth world so that they would agree to help build a new world. After Spider Woman went into the reed, the smallest children followed, then the older children, women carrying their babies, warriors, and husbands. Lastly, Sky Spirit entered the reed for it was his ability to control the air that would transport them all into the fourth world through the Sipapu and into the Kiva. From there, they would disperse into the new land.

"Out of the dead lands, with the help of the spirits and beasts of the fourth world, a new world would be created; a place where they could be at peace with all creatures," Mondoani said, finishing the story.

While she spoke, Mondoani's eyes traveled and watched one girl after another. Completely filled with the energies of Sky Spirit and Spider Woman, she knew intuitively that multiple choices for an apprentice would not be needed as they had been when the Old Mother had chosen her. Mondoani knew this to be true because it had been whispered to her by Spider Woman and Sky Spirit during her telling of the powerful story of the tribe's beginnings here in the fourth world.

Twelve

Still, Mondoani understood she would need to pick many girls and allow the clan to believe it was necessary, for she was just a new memory keeper. This was the tradition and what they all remembered from the times the Old Mother had chosen each of her apprentices.

"It's time for me to sleep young ones; for tomorrow we will have a long day as we travel through the desert. Children, before we find our beds, please, come to me and tell me your names," requested Mondoani.

As the children walked up to her, she looked each one in the eyes, boy and girl, and listened as they introduced themselves. *I should know all their names for I grew up here,* Mondoani thought, wistfully. *But living the secluded life I did with the Old Mother, I missed out on much of what went on in the tribe. As the new memory keeper, I must remain a part of the tribe and not seclude myself or my apprentice.*

As the children and adults went off to bed, Mondoani walked to her belongings and curled up in her own bedroll. Immediately, she fell asleep and the spirits and energy of Spider Woman and Sky Spirit followed into her dreams. There, she saw the face of each of the girls that would stand in line for the testing, though now, she feared that Naomi's heart would be broken: Spider Woman and Sky Spirit had shown her that Ashtra would be chosen.

It did not matter that Ashtra was such a social butterfly. Spider Woman and Sky Spirit called Ashtra, and Mondoani had seen them in the child's eyes. She might have missed seeing the signs if Spider Woman and Sky Spirit had not also filled her own soul. None of the other girls had appeared to sense the pure presence of the great spirits, but Ashtra had. Mondoani knew this for their spirits had touched each other in the powerful wave that was the spirit world.

She had not intended for the spirits of Spider Woman and Sky Spirit to enter into her or into Ashtra. Mondoani did not even understand why these spirits had come, but they had. Many times during her trances, she had been touched by the spirit of the Eagle, the Snake, and of the four elements: Earth, Air, Fire, and Water. She had felt the Thunder Boys, Thunder Spirits, and Tihkuyiwuhti when she called for rain or for the success of the hunt. So many of the spirits had come to her in trance as she had studied under the Old Mother, yet never had she felt any spirit's energy so strongly.

What does it mean? She wondered, still in her dream. *I feel there is a change coming for the tribe and for all of life in the fourth world. If it does not mean that why would the story of leaving the third world and entering into the fourth world have been so important for me to tell? It's not the story I had planned on telling, but it is the story that I told. I must rest, for crossing the arid land tomorrow will be difficult and we must reach the oasis before nightfall or we won't all survive to live another day.*

The choosing must be done in the sacred place before daybreak, when we reach the oasis.

Thirteen

With a gentle nudge of her shoulder, Chief Concierce, woke her before dawn broke. This was unusual, to say the least. He had never done so before. Only in the direst of circumstances had he come to wake the Old Mother, but those times had been few and far between.

His dark braids hung down over his shoulders. Someone had braided the Chief's braids with the feathers of the hawk and the eagle, the teeth of the mountain lion, and bits of turquoise as was tradition for ceremonies but not for a trek through the arid land.

Mondoani did not know what to make of his pre-dawn visit, nor would she ask.

Instead, after taking a sip of water from the cup he handed her, brushing a hand across her eyes, and smoothing her hair, she rose quietly and followed behind.

Concierce led her quietly through the sleeping camp, past the braves standing sentry, and to the edge of the cliff. There, he stopped and stood quietly for a moment looking out into the desert. The moon and stars hung low in the sky. A light breeze brought the scent of the sand and cactus as he motioned for her to stand next to him and spoke.

"Mondoani, I have never heard the story you told the clan last night. Where did you learn it?"

"I learned it at the end just before the Old Mother passed, during the final transfer of her power to me, as is the custom," she answered.

Staring out at the desert, Concierce said, "I felt something different last night during the telling of this story, something powerful that filled my soul with dread and wonder.

What was it?"

"It was the spirits of Spider Woman and Sky Spirit, my chief," Mondoani replied. "I don't know why they chose to come to us last night, just before we begin the hardest hours of our quest; those that take us through the arid land, across the dead land, and through the plains. But, they did. I never knew these spirits before now, and their story is not the one I had intended on telling. However, it is the one that they demanded of me when they entered into me."

"Young Mother," said Concierce.

"Please Sir," she answered, "call me Mondoani. 'Young Mother' was the name of Old Mother when she was a young woman. I am Mondoani."

"I understand, Mondoani," replied the Chief, "and so it shall be.

Naomi, the mother of my children, told me how exhausted you were when you returned last night from casting the Circle of Protection."

"Naomi told you correctly, my Chief," Mondoani said, staring out at the waning moon.

Shuffling his feet, Concierce continued. "She also advised me that you must pick an apprentice and soon. Naomi begged me to request you not pick our daughter, Ashtra, but I fear her wishes cannot come true. Am I right?"

Turning to look at the Chief, Mondoani replied: "Yes, Sir; I believe the Gods have chosen Ashtra. I know tradition requires that many girls are put to the test so that the Gods will be honored, and this will be done. I fear, though, that Spider Woman and Sky Spirit have chosen her already, for something special. We can only hope that this doesn't foretell of something dire.

We can hope that it will bring us instead, to a previously unknown land of plenty."

"Am I right, then, when I say last night they also entered my daughter, young mother?" Concierce asked quietly yet firmly.

Mondoani paused a moment then spoke assuredly, "Yes, Sir, I believe so but the coming days will tell us for sure. Whatever happens, it will be as the Gods wish. That I can promise you, and I believe it will bring changes to our way of life too."

With a nod of his head, Concierce motioned her to turn and follow him back to the camp. He did not speak to her again but left her at the edge of camp and there, he motioned for the guards to wake the rest of the tribe. It was vital that they leave before dawn.

As Mondoani began packing her things, rolling up her bedroll, and re-braiding her hair, she watched the camp.

The women already had the fire going to make tortillas; the beans had been cooking slowly since nightfall and were nearly ready to mash. Whatever was left from this morning's meal would be stored in pottery jars, carried on the sleds that the dogs would pull through the desert.

While she continued to pack, many thoughts about the day ahead tumbled through Mondoani's mind. Their meal at the end of the day, if they made it to the oasis, would be ash cakes – the rolled corn meal would sit in the sand at the edge of the oasis while they built the camp. It would be eaten before bed with bits of beans from their stores. There would not be time to hunt before they reached the oasis and it was forbidden to do so as this was a sacred place. But, if they were lucky, the clan would reach the sanctuary by dusk. If they were not lucky, they would not reach it until after the stars lit the sky.

If that were the case, her people would not eat ash cakes, just a bit of cold beans with maybe a leftover fried tortilla. At dawn in the sacred place at the oasis, the choosing must be done.

Mondoani bundled up her belongings and picked up her staff, continuing to think about the day and all that must be done.

It would only be with luck if the braves were to catch some fish at the water hole, for the time would be short and they must reach the next oasis before the day's end if they were to survive. Though, in the sacred spot, none must hunt or fish. Nothing could be taken but that which was offered by the Gods.

All their meals would be slim until they reached the grasslands. There would be little time to hunt and the women would not have the time to spend cooking; for they must walk.

Each member of the tribe ate quickly and quietly, afraid yet eager to move on.

All were fearful that they would not reach the oasis that night and each sent a silent prayer to the universe for a safe journey.

Fourteen

Brutally the heat from Father Sun beat down on the clan; sweat poured off the men, women, children, and especially the babies carried in cradleboards on their mothers' backs. Although, the women had wrapped the babies in the loosest, coolest swaddling, the heat of the sun was still scorching.

Only a short time into the trek, Concierce called for their water to be rationed. If they ran into any problems that caused delay, each drop saved might mean the difference between life and death for the tribe in this arid land.

Mondoani had taught many the history of the cactus, how to get water from one should it be needed.

But, the further they traveled into these dead lands, the fewer cacti they would find.

The tribe had not had to travel these lands since the Thunder Spirits had left them a few years ago. They knew the Thunder Boys and Thunder Spirits were displeased, yet nothing in the histories could explain why nor how to appease them enough to bring back the rain.

The deep desert had always been difficult to cross, but since the lakes and rivers on the other side of the cliffs had suffered from the loss of water, the desert had become a death trap for many. Even sly foxes and sneaky coyotes avoided most of the deepest parts of the desert. One could still find rattlers, scorpions, and other deadly things, but they usually stayed buried under the sand during the worst of the day.

At night, the scorpions would venture out to kill any prey they could find.

If not for the scorpions and rattlers, the tribe might have crossed in the night.

But time was of the essence if they were to get through the prairie lands before the snows fell. Mondoani had told the tribe about the signs that predicted blizzards and extreme cold would occur this year on the prairie. Such conditions would make traveling even more dangerous for food had become scarce since the Thunder Spirits had brought no rain and, as a result, the worst of the winter's beasts would be a menace as they, too, hunted for food.

As time moved on into the hottest part of the day, Mondoani's braids became slick with sweat. Her leather tunic clung to her, scratching the skin beneath her arms; her tongue was swollen from lack of water.

Still, the tribe pushed on steadily, moving deeper and deeper into the desert until, finally, the sun began to sink from its zenith.

Would they make it? Mondoani wondered, noting how so many now had to assist others to keep moving forward.

Looking towards the horizon in front of the tribe, beyond the Chief, Mondoani thought she saw the oasis, not too far across the desert. *It must be a mirage,* she thought. The tribe had just passed the half-way point, as the sun showed it to be, so the oasis could not be near. *It must be a mirage. If I saw it, others would too,* Mondoani determined and managed to croak out a warning for the runners to go tell Concierce; he would then be prepared to stop his people from running for what had to be a mirage.

Concierce sent out the warning and the braves kept watch not only on the surrounding desert, but also on their own people.

Though the agony from the hot sun and lack of water was fierce, Mondoani's mind continued to try to remember how the choosing was done.

I know how it felt for me when the spirits entered into me at my choosing, but what did I do that enabled the Old Mother to know I was the one? She tried to focus on many possibilities but the act of thinking was now becoming nearly impossible.

Still, Mondoani struggled to think. This much she knew: the choosing must be done in the hallowed site at the oasis. It was imperative that all other Gods and Spirits have their say in who became her apprentice, who would take her place should she die. None must be dishonored.

Even though Sky Spirit and Spider Woman had picked Ashtra, that did not mean that she would be the apprentice chosen. There were so many factors and so many Spirits. Through the years, it had been one spirit or another that had chosen, but there was nothing in the histories about a time when Spider Woman and Sky Spirit had done the choosing.

Wiping her brow, Mondoani mused as memories from the Old Mother filled her. *What would happen if the spirits warred within her for the right to choose?* Memories went back through many generations of memory keepers and one memory caught her attention: it spoke of a time when this had happened. *The memory keeper went mad for a while and, for a few months, no one was chosen; the tribe suffered and dwindled until she was able to once again free herself from the trance.*

After that, an apprentice was finally chosen. Would that happen here? Mondoani wondered, shuddering and then, she stumbled. *I do not know and the unknown is frightening.*

Ashtra was at her shoulder and, immediately, picked her up when she stumbled. Mondoani had not realized Ashtra was there but nodded her thanks.

Ashtra appeared to be thriving in this barren land, her spirit strong, her body straight as she put an arm under Mondoani's shoulder. The young girl's strength helped her to continue on. One of the runners had seen Mondoani fall and handed her the water skin. He held it and let a few drops fall onto her tongue and down her swollen throat. She was given a few more drops until Mondoani felt she could stand on her own. As a thank you, she stroked Ashtra's cheek; it was too hot to touch her further and anything else would delay the tribe.

Mondoani had so many questions for Ashtra but these must wait until they were alone. She wanted to know what Ashtra had felt when Sky Spirit and Spider Woman touched her; and how she managed to appear so unaffected by the climate and barrenness of the land.

Fifteen

Father Sun's splash of color swept across the horizon. The reds, oranges, pinks, and vivid yellows covered the sky, shimmering over the yellow sand making it difficult to see. His beauty was mesmerizing, and yet it was impossible for them to know if they were close enough to the oasis. Out here in the desert, the heat of the sun quickly turned cold once Father Sun had set and night fell. Now that they had crossed so deeply into the desert, not even cacti could be seen growing on the land; it was all rock and a yellow, cracked, arid ground. Soon, the scorpions and other dangerous creatures of the night would come out to hunt. Perhaps, the tribe could find the rest of the way by starlight but Mondoani worried; the moon was only a sliver tonight and a haze that might trick them was coming off the sand.

One of the women stumbled and fell then; she was picked up and carried by one of the braves. Her baby was handed to another woman to carry, and the tribe trekked on.

It was near dusk when those in front finally saw the first trees of the oasis in the distance. No one ran; everyone was spent, only able to stumble forward now and a few of the children were crawling. Everyone, that is, except Ashtra; she stood straight up, seeming to breathe in air that brought her more strength.

Surely Spider Woman and Sky Spirit still held sway in her, decided Mondoani, gazing in admiration at Ashtra. This young girl Mondoani had always thought of as a social, bubble-headed butterfly appeared now to be a rock of strength. In a clear voice, Ashtra spurred on the children so that they would keep moving forward, one more step and then another. Her hair fell in rivers down her back and, in Mondoani's current state of mind, Ashtra took on the appearance of Spider Woman.

The air turned cold as the sun set, leaving just a hint of its glow on the horizon; enough to light up the view of rich greenery in that appeared in front of the tribe. They had made it! As she breathed a sigh of relief, the question that stuck in Mondoani's mind was: *How many would have the strength to move on in the morning? How many of them would be left who would still be able to stand in the predawn air for the choosing?* Mondoani herself was not sure she could do it, yet she knew that she must.

With a great sense of relief, the tribe moved into the oasis itself but kept going forward. First, the camp must be set up though no circle would need to be cast if they set up in the sanctified clearing. Nothing would harm them in this sacred place. Only peace reigned in this place where man, animal, plant, bird, and insect shared the bounty and respected each other. All life could feel the presence of holiness in the land around them.

Both Mondoani and Ashtra felt the peaceful presence before the others, even though they were at the end of the line. Mondoani recognized that Concierce could feel it also, for his back became straighter, his eyes keener, and his step held a spring in it that she had not seen for many a mile. Mondoani looked at each of the members of the tribe and noticed that everyone now stood just a bit taller. The spirits of those who dwell in this revered place gave new strength to the tribe.

Sixteen

When the tribe reached their goal, they slipped the packs off their backs and some untied the dogs; they whined and strained against their bonds until freed then ran to the lake that lay beneath the waterfall. There they leapt into the water, jumping around, splashing, and drinking until, finally, they shook themselves off. Lying down before the newly made fire, the dogs waited for their meal; they would not hunt this night.

Everyone knew their task for making camp; it did not take long. The fires had been built, the corn meal and beans removed from the packs. There would be no meat this night nor in the morning; in this holy place, no one hunted here, no meat was eaten, nor was any plant picked. All that was taken was what was freely given by nature and the Gods. The babies were bathed by the women and they splashed each other, too, while watching the younger children swim and dunk each other. No water ever felt or tasted so delicious to any of the tribe as did the water here, but soon they were sated.

Ashtra sat next to Mondoani throughout their meal and later, side by side, they ministered to those whose skin held the fire of the sun most strongly, massaging soothing aloe into their skin. It seemed to Mondoani as if Ashtra already knew that no choosing would need to be done.

"Mondoani, when you told us the story of Spider Woman and Sky Spirit, something strange happened within me," said Ashtra. "It was different from all those other times I listened to stories. In the past, I could picture the tale when it was woven, but this time it was as if Sky Spirit was talking to me and it felt as if I was Spider Woman. I could feel the heat of the air from the destroyed earth of the third world and sense the wickedness of people who hunted just for the pleasure of the kill. Their devilish nature sickened me and the smell of sulfur from the burning of temples and holy places packed my nostrils. The scent of the dead and dying filled the air, and I knew all that lived in the third world were failing.

I could see Sky Spirit before me, Mondoani, and he filled me with hope and love; and I was heavy with his child. He was the most beautiful creature I have ever seen. Deep within my very bones and soul, I was changed. It's hard to explain but things were different, not as I had always known them to be, nor was I the same girl; I was someone different. During the crossing I was different. Now I am someone who can withstand temperatures higher than I have ever known. I can see further into the past and beyond the now into the future. Yet, Mondoani, the past I see is in the third world, not in this one," Ashtra explained then took a deep breath.

Mondoani gestured with her hand for Ashtra to continue.

"The future lies before me as if there are many roads and I stand at the crossroad, with all the different paths around me. I know things I ought not to know but, at the same time, there are gaps. I don't know what happened between coming into the fourth world and the day I had my first memories in this life. What does it mean, Mondoani? Am I to be your apprentice so I can fill in the gaps or do I have another future in front of me that is heretofore unknown?" she finished, confusion etched on her face.

Mondoani placed a hand on Ashtra's shoulder and replied, "Ashtra, I don't know yet myself. It may, in truth, be some of both. I believe things will change for all of us whether for good or bad; all will be decided by whatever path we take. The histories say that the choosing must happen, and that all the Gods and Spirits must be allowed to have a say in the choosing. I had never heard of a time when Spider Woman and Sky Spirit chose to speak nor heard of a time when they did the

choosing. Even those deepest memories that
transferred into me before the passing of the Old
Mother contained no knowledge of these things.

"I fear, Ashtra, you have aged well beyond
your years in a single night. The transformation
can only be explained by my telling of the story of
Spider Woman and Sky Spirit; it seems their spirits
still abide within you. There is so much I would
like to speak to you about and so much I want to
ask, for you were unaffected by the dead lands;
you seemed to grow stronger the deeper we moved
into them.

But this isn't the time to speak, Ashtra. We
must sleep for the ceremony will take place before
dawn. Afterwards, we must start the second part of
the journey, through the barren land with our only
hope to make the prairie before night falls. Now,
off to your bed, Ashtra, and wake when the call
comes to you. It will be then that the spirits are
gathering for the choosing."

While they were talking, Mondoani watched Naomi looking at her from across the fire. Naomi's eyes contained a new kind of sadness: she knew the daughter of her heart had already moved past her. Ashtra, with all the promise that her beauty and charm held, would not move into an alliance with the Chief from another clan. Ashtra would not bring the tribe more allies, nor would she bear babies that Naomi could spoil, teach, and find joy in. Naomi's heart was sore with yearning though she knew. Mondoani's only hope was that Naomi would not see her as the enemy but, instead, understand that Ashtra was chosen by Spider Woman and Sky Spirit for greatness and to ensure the survival of more than just their tribe.

Mondoani turned her head back as Ashtra stood and leaned to help her up. She stated softly, "Good night, Mondoani. I wish you sweet dreams and a restful sleep, for your day has been hard."

"Good night, dear Ashtra," Mondoani replied and made her way to her sleeping roll.

Seventeen

The stars hung low in the sky, and the moon was hidden from sight; it was the night of the dark moon, a hallowed time. The time of the choosing was at hand. Twenty girls ranging from ages six to thirteen stood in a line waiting. These girls had been called by the spirits of this place. Their hair was braided and decorated with feathers, flowers, and beads. Each child was shivering in the chill of the predawn air, and in anticipation and fear as Mondoani moved around them.

She placed her stones, cup, wand, woven shield, and knife in their place at each of the Four Quarters as she drew the sanctified circle around the young girls. On the outside of the inner circle, Mondoani had woven a larger circle to encompass the entire tribe. They could not cross into the smaller circle but would be blessed and protected. Each in their own way would feel the presence of the spirits as they came one by one to do the choosing, but no one in the tribe would be able to interfere with the choices made by the Gods.

As Mondoani called upon the Quarters – the elements of Earth, Air, Fire, and Water – for both the inner and the outer circles, the spirits began descending. They gathered into the inner circle. She felt the presence of the Thunder Boys and each of the Thunder Gods, first. The spirit of the Eagle landed and Snake slithered in as Selu, the Goddess of the corn arrived. Sky Coyote, who gambled with the other gods, followed then Sotunknang, the nephew of the great Creator. Next came Takuskanskan, the God of change and even Taiowa, the great Creator himself, came into the circle. Mondoani had never felt the presence of so many from the spirit world.

The air was thick with the manifestation of the Gods. She could see some of the younger girls swaying under the combined power of the spirits. Some even appeared to sense that they would be crushed; their essence could not hold in the face of such power. Mondoani felt her own self become smaller as more and more of the spirits entered. Each one examined a girl child and moved on to the next. Sacqua fainted and thus, was no longer able to be chosen. Her spirit was not strong enough for what would be needed. Karenden swayed, faltered, and finally, she too crumbled softly to the ground. Quenth, Basilla, Moretha, Catertna, Drathia, Edwinath, Fatima, and finally Gwenth lay sleeping on the ground at the edge of the circle.

Of the twenty girls, ten had been found to be not suitable to any of the spirits that moved within the circle; the Gods granted them sleep to spare them from madness. In the outer circle, the mothers of these girls were crying. Some wanted to pull their daughters from the inner circle, but were held back by the braves and the spirits guarding the Four Quarters. Some sobbed for they had wished their daughter to be picked, to become an apprentice to the memory keeper; they knew their child's chance of an advantageous marriage was slight.

Ashtra, Zenitha, Tayatha, Norterna, Hermina, Iona, Jarena, Lilith, Opatha, and Portiana still stood, though the latter appeared to be in shock. Of the ten, only Ashtra, Zenitha and Lilith stood strong. Momentarily, the other seven seemed to sway, ready to faint or fall. Mondoani herself felt barely able to breathe. If so many spirits had showed up at her choosing ceremony, she was afraid she would have fainted too. As it was, the heaviness that lay in her grew to nearly unbearable heights as one spirit after another entered into her, blessed her, and helped open her mind into the deeper mysteries. Each planted its kernel of wisdom in her, giving her more knowledge and power.

Just when she thought she could stand no more, it was as if the sea parted for each spirit moved aside within Mondoani, making an aisle for other spirits to come through. Both her inner and

outer eyes were opened. Mondoani watched as two
of the most beautiful beings walked through the
tribe's outer circle. It was Sky Spirit and Spider
Woman.

Sky Spirit shone with an inner light that
glowed, filling the air with twirling silver and gold
particles; and Spider Woman's shiny, long, black
hair hung to her knees, flowing in the breeze,
sometimes covering her body and sometimes
flying out in all directions. A soft silver cloth made
of moon dust clung to her body and her feet
danced over the ground. A tinkle of laughter
followed her, and the sound of chimes sang
sweetly in their wake.

Sky Spirit stopped in the outer circle, first in
front of Concierce, who bowed before him. Sky
Spirit brushed his hand across the Chief's forehead
in blessing before he turned, walked over, and
stood in front of a young dark haired brave named
Towandiaca, which meant Flies Like An Eagle.

Towandiaca swayed a bit and sank to his knees, but Sky Spirit held out his hand and pulled him to his feet. Sky Spirit's voice was strong like thunder yet soft as rain when he spoke. "Spider Woman and I know it is not the time of the choosing of one who will be next in line to be Chief, but it is necessary for these times you are about to enter. After tonight, Towandiaca will be filled with the Spirit of the Sky People. He will be next in line and second in command to our beloved Concierce, who has led this clan with honor, love, hope, knowledge, and intelligence and will continue to do so. But from today on, Towandiaca will learn at his feet, what is needed and how to be a formidable chief. He will hold council with Concierce on all matters for he will have knowledge beyond this lifetime."

With Towandiaca's hand in his, Sky Spirit led him to the Chief. Then he turned to Spider Woman, a smile on his brilliant face and love could be seen in hers. They joined hands and passed through the invisible door into the inner circle. The two headed directly to Ashtra and bowed their heads before her.

Spider Woman gazed lovingly at Ashtra and spoke: "Our daughter's daughter, you are not meant to be a memory keeper's apprentice. Your destiny, though joined with the memory keeper, is also joined with that of Towandiaca. Your children shall bring a new beginning for your clan, and you will travel beyond the fourth world and into the fifth world. When it is time for you to enter the fifth world, the knowledge of the third world and this fourth world will be yours. You, Ashtra, will have knowledge of all the memories from both worlds."

Turning, Spider Woman's hand reached out and brushed the hair from Mondoani's eyes. In a silky voice, she continued: "Ashtra, you will learn from Mondoani who is both wise and magnanimous. It is not our job here to do the choosing of the next memory keeper. Today, we are here to bring forward the children of our children's children many generations removed and cause their spirits to be filled with the spirits of their ancestors. Each will fulfill the need of the other and will be given all the necessary knowledge, for they are our kin not only blood, but in the spirit that resides in them," Spider Woman finished.

Eighteen

Both Spider Woman and Sky Spirit turned and bowed to each of the spirits that filled the circle then reached out and took Ashtra's hands – Sky Spirit her right hand and Spider Woman her left. They led her through the inner circle and out into the outer circle. There, Sky Spirit took Towandiaca's right hand, Spider Woman took Ashtra's left hand and placed joined it with Towandiaca's.

"Towandiaca, I give you the woman, Ashtra, as your mate. You will honor her, cherish her, and listen to her wisdom," Sky Spirit stated in a firm voice.

Spider Woman spoke next: "Ashtra, I give you Towandiaca as your mate.

You will follow him, trust him, honor him, and speak only true wisdom in his ears.

Your eyes will love him and seek him out even in the darkest of times. Your ears will be ever ready to hear his wisdom, for it will be as of the Sky Spirit."

From the two, who were just joined together, flowed a glowing golden light. Neither had words to speak as they stood in front of Concierce, facing Sky Spirit and Spider Woman. Their lives were forever changed and entwined as one. For they had just learned that, one day, they would lead the clan to the Promised Land, into the fifth world. The strength from their spirits flowed back and forth, through one another, as the young man and the young woman were bound in this life and the next.

Concierce laid a hand upon the shoulders of each, looked at Sky Spirit and Spider Woman and smiled. "I will teach them all of my wisdom and care for them until the time is right for them to lead us forth."

"That is all we ask of you great Chief," Sky Spirit said as he bowed his head in acknowledgement of this truth and then, turned back toward the inner circle. Spider Woman and Sky Spirit once again joined hands and stepped back into the inner circle. They walked to Mondoani and placed a gentle hand on her head as each touched their lips to her cheek.

"Do not fear for you will have the best of both worlds now. You will have many apprentices for a time, though one will teach you more than you teach her; one who is from the lineage of Spider Woman, both in spirit and in blood.

We will join our brothers and sisters for the choosing, though we will not make this choice. We will honor the choice, for a new day will dawn soon," Sky Spirit said. Then Spider Woman leaned over and whispered into Mondoani's ears.

"You are also a daughter of my heart and will lead the tribe well. If you need me, call and I will come."

With that the two moved to the side so the Elements of Earth, Air, Water, and Fire could guide the choosing for the next memory keeper's apprentice. Mondoani, hand to her cheek, could still feel the spidery touch of the sweet gentleness and strength of the body that was Spider Woman as well as the steel moonbeam that came from Sky Spirit.

She stood quietly now, empowered with the knowledge that the tribe would be protected and she would have an apprentice, a memory keeper and a teacher.

Each would fill an appropriate need depending upon the times, their sense of awareness, and the circumstances of the day. Mondoani rejoiced in the love that she knew would come from the mating of Ashtra and Towandiaca.

The knowledge and truths that would benefit all of the tribe would also come from their joining, both now and after they came of age. Indeed, a new day was dawning for never before had there been a memory keeper, a second in command, and the son and daughter of Sky Spirit and Spider Woman chosen all on the same day.

Mondoani looked around then. Still standing in line was the last of the girls: Zenitha, Tayatha, Norterna, Hermina, Iona, Jarena, and Lilith.

The other two had joined their friends on the ground, fast asleep dreaming, for their spirits were not strong enough to handle the depth of the energies that spread toward them.

Nineteen

Mondoani stood up straight and began her chant. It was the beginning of the choosing ceremony and, even though Sky Spirit and Spider Woman had said that the elements would do the choosing this season, all must be made ready. Each of the Gods, Spirits, and Elements must be given honor and allowed their role.

Mondoani spoke: "On this moonless night in the sanctified oasis, I honor all who share this space with me and all who were not called to come." She bent and picked up a bit of the earth from between her feet. "Mother Earth, I beseech you to bless us with someone who will aid me in healing the land." From the pouch that hung on the leather tie around her neck, she pulled a piece of sage and walked to the fire pit in the center of the circle. "Father Fire, I ask you to shine kindly upon the land – not so hot as to scorch us nor so cold as to freeze the land – to help consecrate this choosing with the one who will be blessed with the ability to smell evil before it strikes and warn us," she said as she lit the sage and walked around the perimeter of the circle. "Father Air, I beseech you to bless us with cool breezes in the heat and clean air to breathe. I ask for your help so that one can be chosen who will be able to smell the seasons upon the air and know when the time to move is at hand."

Then Mondoani stopped near the waterfall. From the lake near her feet, she dipped and filled a cup. Bringing it to her lips, she drank a small amount and then sprinkled the perimeter of the inner circle. As she walked, she intoned, "Mother Water, I beseech you to bless our tribe with plenty of fresh water and rain to ripen and feed the crops. I ask that you help in the choosing so that our tribe can always be water rich, and so that the one that is chosen will have the ability to see the past, present, and future.

"I beseech all spirits who wish to take part in this choosing to bless our clan and the land we walk upon; to choose one who will both aid me and teach me so that we can learn together the best means to protect our people, the land, and all life that grows, walks, flies, crawls, or swims. Please know that, as memory keeper, I, Mondoani, understand that I am only a part of the plan and am open to receive help in honoring each of you in your proper seasons and at the proper times."

After giving honor to the Four Quarters, Mondoani took her place in front of the young women and called out, "Spirits great and small, those who are here and those who chose to aid us in the choosing, I honor you. I ask you now for a sign that I may know your will. I ask you to choose one of these girls to be my apprentice, helper, and friend; someone who, some day, will carry on after I have passed over the bridge and into the Summerland."

Mondoani stood with arms spread wide in order to allow spirits to enter into her being if they deemed it necessary for the choosing. There was nothing more she could do now except wait.

Twenty

A breeze flowed through the circle, stirring the earth around them. The smell of sage floated through the air and droplets of water splashed them from the nearby lake that now surrounded them. A magical tide had appeared, brought in by the water sprite and surrounded the hill upon which the inner and outer circles had been cast. The tribe stood on a hill upon an island now.

Zenitha, Tayatha, Norterna, Hermina, Iona, Jarena, and Lilith stood in front of Mondoani, in a half circle waiting. None looked at anything. All stood as if at peace with life, breathing in the scent of sage, feeling the drops of water with the air weaving in and out and the earth under their feet. They all sensed the presence of each of the Elements, Spirits, and Gods.

For a moment, Mondoani feared none would be chosen, that all would be found wanting; but then Iona cried out and swooned. Norterna wailed and faltered as Hermina keened and sunk to her knees. Next, Jarena moaned and slid slowly down to land on the soft grass that had sprung beneath her feet. Tayatha cried out as she, too, dropped gently to land on the grass then fell fast asleep with her head pillowed on Jarena, best friends even now. Only two stood: Zenitha, a tall brunette with a nose and mouth a bit large for her face but, otherwise, pretty; and Lilith, small for her age but strong of spirit – what she lacked in height and physical strength, she made up in beauty and a shy sweetness.

Each of the Elements, in their own unique ways, blessed the girls as they stood. The wind picked up and blew through the fire, causing the flames to flick higher. The smell of sage filled the air more strongly. It began to rain but not a hard rain, more of a sprinkle. Neither one of the girls gave way. Both entered a state of bliss as their spirits filled with energy from the Four Elements.

Lilith spread her arms wide to accept water into her spirit and buried her toes into the earth beneath her feet until they were covered in mud. Zenitha's arms reached for the sky, moving in concert with the wind. She inhaled deeply the smell from the burning wood and basked in the warmth of the fire; her nose quivered, embracing the smell of fresh air. Something extraordinarily memorable was happening and all who were there that night in the holiest of places knew it.

Two had been chosen: one to carry the spirits of water and earth and the other to hold the spirits of air and fire: all of life needed these four elements. Neither the Thunder Boys and the Thunder Gods, nor the snakes, coyotes, eagles, or any life could exist without the Four Elements. For the first time in the memory of the third and fourth worlds, there was to be a memory keeper and two apprentices. One day, those two apprentices would become memory keepers and the tribe would have three for a while if all lived. Truly, they were blessed this night.

Mondoani stood in awe for a moment, taking it all in then turned to the spirits that shared this space with the tribe. She thanked them for the honor they had bestowed on her and the tribe. She humbly expressed her gratitude for their help and then, slowly sank to her knees. Mondoani was so spent; never before to her knowledge had anyone held within them the spirits of so many Gods, all at one time. She had two circles to close and still must honor each of those that joined them before she could retire. But she was spent.

First to leave were Sky Spirit and Spider Woman, who stopped and kissed her and each of the new memory keepers on their foreheads. In the outer circle, they held Ashtra for a moment in their arms and patted Towandiaca on his shoulder. The other spirits began to depart: up into the sky flew Eagle. With a roll of thunder and a crack of lightening, Eagle was followed by all of the

Thunder Gods and the Thunder Boys. Selu, the Goddess of the corn, disappeared leaving only corn dust in her wake, and Sky Coyote, who did not gamble that night, trotted off into the trees. Sotunknang, the nephew of the great Creator, Takuskanskan the God of change, and even Taiowa left quietly with only a hollow echo heard with their going.

The four elements remained for it was the custom of the people to honor, thank, and release them. Never before had Mondoani felt that she had so much to be thankful for. She sat upon her knees for a moment and prayed. Zenitha and Lilith almost in unison lowered their arms and turned first to each other, recognizing the magnificent gift that had been bestowed upon them. After throwing their arms around each other and burying their heads for a second upon the other's shoulder, they looked up and stepped towards the memory keeper.

With great care, Zenitha and Lilith lifted
Mondoani to her feet and placed their arms around
her. As one, the three bowed deeply to the
Elements of Earth, Air, Fire, and Water. Tonight,
no more words needed to be said for all of the
Spirits and Gods felt they, too, had been blessed
with something that had never happened before
and might never happen again.

Air and Fire flew off. As Water sank into the
Earth, the lake disappeared and Water and Earth
became one. Without additional ceremony, both
circles had opened and the tribe descended the hill
to the camps. Celebrations would need to wait and
would come after the tribe reached the sea.

Mondoani's exhausted body swayed and she
slumped to the ground, though her spirit was full
and her heart light. Zenitha and Lilith came
running to her side once again, sank down beside
her and gathered Mondoani up into their arms. Her
head lay upon Lilith's lap and Zenitha held her
hand, willing health and strength back into her

limbs, into her body. So depleted was Mondoani when the spirits left her that she had succumbed into sleep. It did not take long, though, so after a short rest, Mondoani awoke and her new apprentices helped her sit up. "Sit here upon the earth while we gather the tools from the Four Quarters and then we will all walk to the camp together," Zenitha stated.

Zenitha moved to the points between the elements of Air and Fire while Lilith made her way between the points of Earth and Water. Each young woman held within her arms the precious tools that were used to mark the Quarters.

At Mondoani's feet, the two young women sat and took the pouch. With care, they placed the sacred tools into their woven wrappings and then, helped Mondoani to her feet. No longer did they stand upon an island; the water had receded, and the oasis was theirs for the night.

Using the white birch staff she had made that spring for Old Mother, Mondoani and her two apprentices walked out together to join the tribe.

This story is dedicated to the remembrance of history and cultures around the world.

You can find out more about this author at:

www.martamoranbishop.com

www.ingramcontent.com/pod-product-compliance
Lightning Source LLC
Chambersburg PA
CBHW052004220626
47052CB00004B/1088

* 9 7 8 1 9 3 9 4 8 4 2 7 7 *